Skip to My Lou

W9-AIA-530

Skip to My Lou

adapted and illustrated by

Nadine Bernard Westcott

SCHOLASTIC INC.
New York Toronto London Auckland Sydney
Mexico City New Delhi Hong Kong

To my mother and father

No part of this publication may be reproduced in whole or in part, or stored in a retrieval system, or transmitted in any form or by any means, electronic, mechanical, photocopying, recording, or otherwise, without written permission of the publisher. For information regarding permission, write to Joy Street / Little, Brown and Company (Inc.), 34 Beacon Street, Boston, MA 02108.

ISBN 0-590-98050-5

Illustrations copyright © 1989 by Nadine Bernard Westcott. All rights reserved. Published by Scholastic Inc., 555 Broadway, New York, NY 10012, by arrangement with Joy Street / Little, Brown and Company (Inc.).
SCHOLASTIC and associated logos are trademarks and/or registered trademarks of Scholastic Inc.

18 17 16 15 14   03 04 05 06

Printed in the U.S.A.

Skip to My Lou

Chorus

Lou, Lou, skip to my Lou, Lou, Lou, skip to my Lou,

Lou, Lou, skip to my Lou, Skip to my Lou, my dar - ling!

Musical notation of "Skip to My Lou" from *Singing Bee!* by Jane Hart. Musical arrangement Copyright © 1982 by Jane Hart. By permission of Lothrop, Lee & Shepard (A Division of William Morrow & Co., Inc.).

Sitting on the front porch,
Painted like new —
The farm's all in order,
There's not much to do.

"Take care of the farm.
We'll be back by two!"

Skip to my Lou, my darling!

Flies in the sugarbowl,

Shoo fly shoo.

Cats in the buttermilk,

Two by two.

Pigs in the parlor,
What'll I do?

Skip to my Lou, my darling!

Cows in the kitchen,
Moo cow moo.

Roosters in the pantry,

Cock-a-doodle-do.

Sheep in the bathtub,

Hulla-baloo!

Skip to my Lou, my darling!

Lou, Lou, skip to my Lou,
Lou, Lou, skip to my Lou,

Lou, Lou, skip to my Lou,
Skip to my Lou, my darling!

Look at the clock,
It's a quarter to two!
Goodness gracious,
What will we do?

Hurry, quick! It's up to you!

Skip to my Lou, my darling!

Phew!